THE FARM SUMMER
1942

Donald Hall

THE FARM SUMMER
1942

Pictures by Barry Moser

DIAL BOOKS New York

Published by Dial Books
A Division of Penguin Books USA Inc.
375 Hudson Street
New York, New York 10014

Text copyright © 1994 by Donald Hall
Pictures copyright © 1994 by Barry Moser
Designed by Barry Moser
Printed in the U.S.A.
First Edition
1 3 5 7 9 10 8 6 4 2

Library of Congress Cataloging in Publication Data
Hall, Donald, 1928–
The farm summer 1942 / by Donald Hall ;
pictures by Barry Moser.
p.   cm.
Summary: A young boy spends the summer on his
grandparents' farm in New Hampshire while his mother
works in the war effort in New York and his father serves on
a destroyer in the Pacific.
ISBN 0-8037-1501-3.—ISBN 0-8037-1502-1 (lib. bdg.)
[1. Grandparents—Fiction. 2. Farm life—New
Hampshire—Fiction.
3. World War, 1939–1945—United States—Fiction.]
I. Moser, Barry, ill. II. Title.
PZ7.H14115Far   1994 [Fic]—dc20   92-38613   CIP   AC

The illustrations for this book were painted with transparent watercolor on
paper handmade for the Royal Watercolor Society by Simon Green. They were
then color-separated and reproduced as red, blue, yellow, and black halftones.

To Peter Olsen Hall

D. H.

For my good friend, Diane Fernald

B.M.

P E T E R lived in San Francisco with his mother while his father was gunnery officer on a destroyer in the United States Navy, fighting in the war faraway in the South Pacific.

A long blue Packard took Peter to school every morning. His mother, who taught mathematics at a university, made cocoa when Peter came home from school. They talked about the war, and when Peter's father might come home on leave.

In the summer of 1942 the government asked Peter's mother to spend the summer in New York, working on a secret project. While his mother worked for the war effort, Peter would help his grandparents on the New Hampshire farm where his father had grown up.

His mother's war work got them tickets on a huge DC-3 airliner, flying from California to New York at one hundred and seventy miles an hour—coast to coast in only sixteen hours!

Then his mother took a streamliner with Peter from Manhattan to Boston and they rode in a taxi across town to North Station where a steam locomotive would carry Peter from Boston up to New Hampshire. His mother asked the conductor to let Peter know when the train stopped at Gale.

The locomotive smoked and chugged north out of the city, past smaller cities, past little towns, into the open countryside. Then the train slowed down and pulled to a stop at a small wooden building with a sign that said Gale.

"Here's your stop," said the conductor to Peter. "Gale's your depot."

Peter stepped down from the train to meet his grandfather.

His grandfather wore overalls, a blue cap, and whispered into the ear of a white horse named Lady Ghost.

Lady Ghost pulled them in the buggy along the road past old farmhouses to a long white house with green shutters where his grandmother waited with gingersnaps and rhubarb pie.

His grandparents' kitchen had a huge black cast-iron stove that burned wood. Peter had never seen such a thing.

His grandfather showed him where the bathroom was, with plumbing fixtures bought by mail from Sears Roebuck, that took the place of the outhouse they used when Peter's father was a boy.

His grandmother showed him how water came out of the faucet from the well uphill, instead of the hand pump beside the sink they used when Peter's father was a boy.

Before bed his grandfather ate milk toast and his grandmother sipped Moxie, which was a strange soft drink that tasted bitter.

Peter didn't like it. Instead he drank a glass of milk that his grandfather brought down from the barn. His grandfather told him that this milk was fresh, warm from the cow—real milk, not pasteurized. It didn't taste like San Francisco milk.

That night Peter slept in the featherbed that his father slept in when he was a boy, under a patchwork quilt made by his great-grandmother—his grandmother told him—out of scraps from his great-great-grandmother's dresses, with a hot-water bottle because it was cold for June.

In the morning his grandfather introduced him to Bertha, Sally, Dottie, Lucy, Drusilla, and Mary Beth.

While he milked in the tie-up, his grandfather told Peter stories about long ago, before cars and airplanes. He recited a poem about a man who jumped and ran away when he saw his first railway train.

His grandmother introduced Peter to the chickens.

When his grandmother stuck her hand under a hen, the hen flew up in the air *squawking squawking squawking* and Peter jumped—like the man afraid of trains—until he saw his grandmother smiling with an egg in her hand.

The next day his grandfather took him to fetch a load of hay in the hayrack.

After his grandfather pitchforked hay into the hayrack, he showed Peter how to rake up loose strands with the bullrake, the way Peter's father used to.

He showed Peter how to feed Lady Ghost a lump of sugar.

On the way back they needed to cross the railroad track and they waited and waited while a long freight-train pulled past them— Peter's grandfather counted ninety-seven cars—taking airplane fuselages and searchlights up to Montreal for shipping to England.

When his grandfather asked Peter how he liked haying, Peter said he liked it—but the hay dust made his head itch.

His grandmother found Peter a straw hat hanging on a peg in the toolshed that Peter's father wore when *he* "raked-after." His grandfather said that when he wore his straw hat, Peter looked just like his father.

That night they drank milk and Moxie, and ate milk toast and listened to Gabriel Heatter on the big radio near the wood stove. Gabriel Heatter's deep voice told about air raids in Europe and fighting in New Guinea.

Peter wore his straw hat while he sat listening.

Peter missed his father.

Peter missed his mother and he missed his friends in San Francisco. But he loved his grandmother's gingersnaps and his grandfather's stories.

And he loved the railroad, twelve trains a day.

The next day they brought salt for the sheep to lick.

The day after, Peter's grandfather needed to go to Andover, four miles away, to talk to a man about selling some timber. They backed Lady Ghost into the carriage and started off. When they drove through a covered bridge, Peter's grandfather told him how in winter the town shoveled snow right onto the bridge—so that sleighs could slide through it.

Halfway to Andover they stopped at a farm so that Peter could play with Emily, who was his age—and the only other nine-year-old for miles around.

Emily showed Peter her dollhouse. Peter was polite; he *liked* the tiny furniture.

Then in Emily's room he found a rubber ball. Emily was polite; they threw it back and forth until Peter's grandfather and Lady Ghost came to pick him up.

On the way back his grandfather showed him the graveyard where Peter's great-great-great grandfather was buried, who fought in the American Revolution against the king of England!

They stopped at Paul Pillsbury's post office and store. Paul thought Peter had grown a whole inch since the night he stepped off the train.

His grandfather bought Peter two chocolate-covered cherries for one penny.

Sundays at church he saw his cousins Edna, Martha, Lucille, Charlie, Clarence, and Audrey, who were big girls and boys, and his cousins Mabelle, Josie, Forrest, and Grant who were grown-ups.

Sunday nights they hitched Lady Ghost to the buggy again and went back to church for Christian Endeavor, which is what they called it when the young people sang hymns.

Peter found "Life Is Like a Mountain Railroad" in the hymnbook. Because Peter loved railroads, every week the young people sang "Life Is Like a Mountain Railroad."

Over the Fourth of July weekend, his mother took the train up from Manhattan.

When his mother stepped off the train at the depot, Peter was rubbing Lady Ghost's ear. His mother hugged him. She kept saying how tall he was. She liked the way Peter looked wearing his father's straw hat.

Peter introduced her to the cows, the chickens, and the sheep. He showed her how to feed Lady Ghost a lump of sugar.

Sundays they didn't hay because it was the Sabbath and Peter's grandmother served cold food because it was wrong to cook on the Sabbath and old friends came calling in the afternoon.

Peter listened to stories about the blizzard of '88 when his grandfather was a boy. Uncle Gene told how they rolled the snow after that blizzard, with an ox pulling the snow-roller that smoothed the snow for sleighs to slide over. But their ox got his hoof stuck in something—and it was the chimney of a house!

Peter saw his grandfather grinning. Peter laughed.

For weeks it didn't rain and that was good because the hay never spoiled and they could hay every day except Sunday.

Then it was *too* dry and the hay turned brown and they hauled water to the beans and corn and squash in the garden.

The hayrack's wooden wheels were so dry, they shrank and the iron rims rattled.

One day when they were rolling downhill with the hayrack full, a rim worked loose—and it rolled right past Lady Ghost. The next morning Peter and his grandfather led Lady Ghost, pulling the hayrack, into the creek to swell the wood inside the iron rims.

Then it rained four days in August and they stayed inside because they couldn't hay in the rain. But the new grass, coming up where they had already cut the hay, turned bright green.

While it rained, Peter's grandfather sat on the chopping block in the woodshed whittling new teeth for the bullrake.

While it rained, Peter found a stack of books in the attic that had been his father's when his father was a boy.

Peter read *Tom Swift and his Flying Machine*. What would Tom Swift have thought of a DC-3?

When they went back to haying, it was cool and maple branches started to turn red.

Peter didn't want the New Hampshire summer to end.

He didn't want to stop feeding chickens and salting sheep.

He liked stories and gingersnaps.

He didn't want to leave Lady Ghost and go home to San Francisco—*but also*

he wanted to fly on a DC-3 again and go home to San Francisco

and live with his mother again and ride to school in a blue Packard

and tell his friends about haying with Lady Ghost

and about a wood stove and a Sears Roebuck bathroom

and cows and sheep and chickens...

and maybe his father would come home on leave from the Navy.

Gabriel Heatter told them about American troops invading a Pacific island called Guadalcanal "with the support of the gallant boys of the United States Navy."

Peter was proud of his father on a destroyer in the Pacific. Peter wanted the war to be over.

The day before Peter took the train back to Boston, he fed the chicks, grown into pullets and almost hens, he helped his grandfather hay, he listened to his grandfather's stories, milking the cows in the tie-up, and watched his grandmother make baked beans and brown bread for supper with string bean salad and fresh corn.

Peter began to wonder if his grandmother and grandfather might surprise him with ice cream for dessert, when he heard a carriage pull into the dooryard—and a Model A and an old Chevy truck.

It was Martha and Charlie and Edna and Clarence and Audrey and Lucille from church, and Emily too, with her older brother Sam on leave from the Marines.

They brought ice cream that Edna and Clarence had cranked themselves and a cake that said *Good-Bye Peter Come Back* and a patchwork quilt to take back to San Francisco to remember New Hampshire by.

Then Edna led everybody singing, "Life Is Like a Mountain Railroad."

Peter said good-bye to Bertha, Sally, Dottie, Lucy, Drusilla, and Mary Beth and the chickens and the hens and the sheep and his grandmother and his grandfather and Lady Ghost and hung his straw hat on its peg in the toolshed.

On the DC-3 flying home at one hundred and seventy miles an hour, Peter's mother told him that his father would come home soon for a whole week before going back to his destroyer.

Peter was happy, going home.

Peter was also sad, missing Lady Ghost and thinking of his straw hat hanging on its peg.

Then his mother told him that probably next summer they would ask her back to New York. Would he like to feed Lady Ghost more lumps of sugar?

Peter was excited driving home from the airport in a taxi through traffic, uphill to their house…

and then the door opened.